ONE

My name is Xer—

Xerxes paused as he recalled his first day at his new school.

Boisterous boys had yelled in his face.

'Xerox! Hey, Xerox!'

'Hey, Xerox what's your surname—Xero?'

Pushing aside the memory of their taunts, he finished writing his name in the first page of his new notebook.

My name is Xerxes Noshir Wadia

His father, Noshir, ran a bakery-cum-café. Xerxes loved spending time there, sitting in the cosy warmth of the café and inhaling its smells of old wood and baking.

Xerxes wrote carefully in his notebook.

My father, Noshir Wadia, runs a bakery. My mother, Sonji Wadia, is a vetary

Xerxes rubbed out the last word, then wrote again, rubbed, wrote, rubbed, wrote, till with a sigh he finally wrote,

My mother, Sonji Wadia is a pet trainer. I study at St

Xerxes pictured himself in different school uniforms and badges—St Alban, St Henry, Ava Petit, Jeejebhoy High—as Sonji towered over him, saying: 'You're going to a better school to help improve your grades!'

Xerxes looked down at his latest badge and wrote the name of the school.

I study at Paranjyot Academy.

I stay at

He shut his eyes trying to recall the twisty metal letters—*Chez Wadia*—on the name plate that hung on the gate of their home. Sonji had explained it to him. 'Chez is French for "in" as in "I stay in" …'

I stay at Chez Wadia. When I grow up I want to be like my Mamavaji.

He glanced at the photo frame on the desk. His parents, Noshir and Sonji, stood stiffly behind

FLYING WITH
GRANDPA

Read more for younger readers

Book of Beasts by M. Krishnan
Monster Garden by Jerry Pinto and Priya Kuriyan
Kittu's Very Mad Day by Harshikaa Udasi
Manya Learns to Roar by Shruthi Rao
The Stupendous Timetelling Superdog by Himanjali Sankar
Missing: A Magnificent Superdog by Himanjali Sankar
Moin and the Monster by Anushka Ravishankar
Moin the Monster Songster by Anushka Ravishankar
Razia and the Pesky Presents by Natasha Sharma
Shah Jahan and the Ruby Robber by Natasha Sharma
Ashoka and the Muddled Messages by Natasha Sharma
Raja Raja and the Swapped Sacks by Natasha Sharma
Akbar and the Tricky Traitor by Natasha Sharma

FLYING WITH
GRANDPA

Madhuri Kamat
Illustrated by Niloufer Wadia

duckbill

To my mother, Saraswati Kamat who said she'd read my story when it's in print. Here it is...
To my father, Shrinath Kamat who got my first manuscript typed on the paper he used for his legal briefs. You got me here...

Duckbill Books

F2 Oyster Operaa, 35/36 Gangai Street,
Kalakshetra Colony,
Besant Nagar, Chennai 600090
www.duckbill.in
platypus@duckbill.in

First published by Duckbill Books 2018

10 9 8 7 6 5 4 3 2 1

ISBN: 978-93-87103-12-2

Typeset by PrePSol Enterprises Pvt. Ltd.

Printed at Thomson Press (India) Ltd.

Also available as an ebook

Children's reading levels vary widely. The general reading levels are
indicated by colour on the back cover. There are
three levels: younger readers, middle readers and young
adult readers. Within each level, the position of the dot
indicates the reading complexity. Books for young
adults may contain some slightly mature material.

Xerxes who was seated on an old man's lap. Xerxes underlined the word 'Mamavaji', then craned his neck to glance at the old man seated in the adjoining room, watching a film on television. On the screen, he could see an alien creature walking backwards.

Xerxes almost fell off his chair as his notebook was suddenly snatched away. Sonji loomed over him, looking furious as she saw the page.

'How untidy you are, Xerxes! Can you not write without rubbing endlessly! And what is this? I'm not a pet trainer. I'm a vet—a veterinary doctor who treats sick animals. You know that. Why did you write pet trainer?'

'I didn't know the spelling.'

'I taught you, Xerxes. Why can't you say it aloud, then you will get the spelling. Repeat after me—V-E-T ...'

Sonji's eyes fell on the last line.

'Mamavaji?! You can't write that you want to be like your Grandpa!'

Sonji tore out the page neatly, sharpened a pencil and handed Xerxes the notebook.

'What will you write, "When I grow up I want to be ..."?'

'A dog trainer.'

'Don't act smart! Write "I want to be like JRD Tata."'

'Look, Mama, Grandpa wants to be like Alien!'

Sonji looked out of the window and saw Grandpa jumping backwards on the pathway outside their home, his arms windmilling as if to give him momentum.

Sonji darted out and looking around quickly to see if her neighbour Preeti was watching, she pulled Grandpa back into the house.

TWO

The following day, Xerxes had to do a Show & Tell in school, on the camera. Sonji made him do some last-minute rehearsing before he left.

Noshir was cooking a meal to pack for Xerxes in his tiffin box.

Sonji put a small polaroid camera into his schoolbag and hurried him out as she glanced at the clock.

'Go and wait for the school bus so that it doesn't drive away. I'll come and give you your tiffin and bag.'

Sonji dashed into the kitchen to collect the tiffin from Noshir and, grabbing the school bag, went out to Xerxes. She stopped short.

Xerxes was jumping backwards from the gate to the kerb, where he was waiting for the school bus.

Sonji rushed forward.

'What do you think you're doing? Do you want to fall? Don't be childish! No one would believe you're going to have your Navjote in a few days!' She turned Xerxes around to face the road. 'Stand still now,' she said sternly.

She hoisted his schoolbag on his back and tucked in his tiffin.

When the school bus arrived, Xerxes remained rooted to the spot like a statue.

Sonji prodded him towards the bus, but he stubbornly refused to move.

'Get in the bus, Xerxes,' Sonji scolded.

'You only told me to stand still!'

The teacher in the bus saw Sonji trying to make Xerxes get in. She came to the door and pulled him in.

'Sorry, sorry to have kept you waiting!' Sonji called out to the teacher as the bus gathered speed.

Xerxes did not turn to wave goodbye to Sonji.

He was still sulking when Sonji picked him up after school.

'How did the Show & Tell go, Xerxes?' Sonji asked as they drove home together.

Xerxes refused to answer and Sonji didn't press him, seeing his grumpy mood. On reaching home, Xerxes went straight to Grandpa's room. He found him trying on the cap bought for his Navjote ceremony.

'I have something to show you,' Grandpa said, when he saw Xerxes. He pulled out an old family album and started showing Xerxes the photographs.

Xerxes saw a little girl with downcast eyes wearing a velvet cap and white dress standing with a young man.

'Who is the girl, Grandpa?'

'Identify me in the photograph and you'll know!'

Xerxes looked at it closely.

'I can't see you anywhere in it, Grandpa.'

'Look again.'

Xerxes was puzzled. The only adult in the photograph looked very young. He traced his fingers over the photograph, then looked back at Grandpa.

'That's you, Grandpa?! But how can that be?'

'Why not?'

'I always think of you as old!'

'Oh, well, I was not always old and bald, you know! I was young, too!'

Grandpa pointed to the little girl in the velvet cap and white robes.

'So then, who is this?'

Xerxes clapped his hands and laughed.

'Mama!'

'Correct!'

'Mama looks so nice, all shy!'

'What's that supposed to mean?'

'Mama's so different now. She's fierce and determined. Not at all shy!' He made a fierce face to show how his mother looked now. When he glanced up, he saw Grandpa had raised himself to his full height and was glowering down at him. 'I was just saying, Grandpa!' said Xerxes, quickly.

'I will not hear needless comments about my daughter; do you hear me loud and clear, young man?'

Xerxes looked sheepish. He'd never seen Grandpa with such a stern expression.

'Sorry, Grandpa.'

'As you should well be! There's nothing wrong with being fierce and determined or with being shy, for that matter! Both are nice!'

'Yes, Grandpa.'

At that very moment, Sonji called out. 'Xerxes, the printed cards for your Navjote have arrived.'

Xerxes rushed out to see them. He held them in his hand and smelt them.

'Do you like them?'

'Yes, Mama, they're so beautiful. And they smell nice!'

'Do you want to invite your class?'

Xerxes thought about it. Maybe his classmates would stop making fun of him when they saw him at his Navjote, in his fine red velvet cap and whiter-than-white new clothes.

So, when Sonji handed him a bunch of invites, he promptly took them.

'Thank you, Mama.' He turned to go, and then turned back. 'The Show & Tell went well,' he said.

Sonji nodded, pleased. She would have liked to know more but Xerxes had already dashed back to Grandpa.

'Grandpa, will you help me write the invitations to my friends?' he asked, excitedly.

Grandpa nodded, smiling.

As Xerxes called out the names of his classmates, Grandpa scrawled them on the invites. But the pen kept slipping from his grasp.

'We'll do it together, Grandpa!' said Xerxes.

Xerxes wrapped his fingers around Grandpa's, and they both wrote out the names on the invites.

'You're all invited to my Navjote,' Xerxes told his classmates in school the next day.

He paused, waiting for questions, but there were none.

'Do you want to know what Navjote is?'

'No, we don't give a jot for what is Navjote!'

Xerxes continued as if he had not heard the comment.

'It means "new worshipper of God" and there is a ceremony where I'll be ...'

The rest of his sentence was drowned out by

a bunch of boys singing aloud. They deliberately mispronounced 'Navjote' as they sang.

We don't give a jot,
we don't give a jot
about Nav Jot!

They chanted louder as he raised his voice to be heard over their din.

'... publicly initiated into the faith that we Parsis follow. Please come.'

As he went around the classroom to place the invitations on each of their desks, one of the boys opened the lid of his desk and let the card slide to the floor. Many of the other boys promptly did the same.

When the teacher came in, they quickly picked them up but tossed them into their desks without looking at them.

THREE

On the day of the Navjote, Xerxes kept looking towards the door of the hired hall where it was being held. Sonji guessed the reason.

'Your classmates will come, perhaps they'll be late. It's a Sunday, after all.'

The Navjote ceremony got over, and the lunch as well.

'Nobody turned up, Mama,' said Xerxes sadly.

'Oh, they may have had other things to do, but see how many presents you've got. Your Papa's overloaded!'

Xerxes saw Noshir's arms were full of presents.

'Why don't you help him with the rest and then you can open them all at home with Mamavaji.'

Xerxes brightened up and ran to help his father.

Back home, Grandpa arranged all the presents in order of size.

'Which do you want to open first, Xerxes?'

'The BIG ones!'

Xerxes eagerly opened the big presents one after another. But there were only books.

'I thought they'd be toys!'

'Maybe the small ones are toys. Let's open and see, shall we?'

Grandpa opened up the smaller gifts.

'They're all envelopes.'

He handed them over to Xerxes. Each of them contained a small booklet. Xerxes took them out.

'What are these, Grandpa?'

'Read out what's written.'

'Gift vouchers. But for what are they?'

'Let me see.'

Grandpa took them and read the headings.

'These are also for books.'

Xerxes started howling. Sonji and Noshir came running. Sonji glared at Grandpa.

'I didn't do anything! He just started crying!'

Noshir took Grandpa out of the room, leaving Sonji with the still wailing Xerxes.

'I want toys, not books!'

'You like books, Xerxes. I suggested books when people asked me what they could gift you on your Navjote.'

'You always give me books so how would you know I don't like toys?!'

'Will you stop shouting!'

'You also shout at me!'

Noshir came back in and told Sonji he would handle Xerxes. Sonji sighed and left, shaking her head in resignation.

'That is no way to speak to your mother! You've already forgotten what you were taught: humate, hukhate, huravaste—good words, good thoughts, good deeds! You can have dinner alone!'

Noshir left the room, shutting the door behind him.

Xerxes put his head down on his arms and started sniffling.

'It is my Navjote and no one from my class came to admire my new clothes. No one gave me what I wanted. Papa also got angry with me. He also didn't buy me toys. Everyone is always getting angry with me but why can't I be angry?' he muttered to himself between sniffles.

Then he sat up and gave himself a little smack on his cheek.

'Didn't you hear what Papa said, be good. Be good,' he told himself.

He said a little prayer.

'May Ahura Mazda please forgive me for not showing gratitude for all the many presents I got.' He paused for a moment. 'But I would really like some Big Toys.'

He heard a knock. A matchbox attached to a string appeared under his door. He put the matchbox to his ear.

'Hello, hello, Grandpa calling Xerxes!'

It was Grandpa, with another matchbox to his ear, on the other side.

'Hello Grandpa,' said Xerxes, in a low voice.

'Why so sad, Xerxes?'

'I want Big Toys.'

'I am your Big Toy.'

'What are you saying, Grandpa?'

Sonji, bringing Xerxes his dinner, saw Grandpa with the matchbox to his ear.

'Xerxes is being punished. No talking. He stays in the room till he says sorry!'

Grandpa mumbled, 'Sorry.'

Sonji's eyes turned moist.

'No, no, Xerxes has been bad. Not you. You don't have to say sorry, Papa.'

As his mother entered with his dinner, Xerxes said 'Sorry' in a small voice.

'All right, Xerxes, come and join us at the table but only after you've put away all the books neatly.'

As he put away the books, Xerxes found a book with photographs. He read the title aloud.

'*The Life of JRD Tata in Pictures.*'

FOUR

Sonji was treating her neighbour Preeti Tulsiani's pooch in her clinic, when she enquired about Xerxes.

'What was all that yelling, Sonji? Everything all right with your son, no?'

'Oh, yes,' mumbled Sonji. 'He was just upset no one in his class turned up for his Navjote.'

'New school, so it will take time for him to make new friends.'

To change the topic, Sonji enquired about Preeti's business.

'So, have you found a place for your organic grocery store?'

'No, the rents are too steep. I'm thinking of converting the garage into my shop as you've done for this clinic.'

Sonji busied herself with the pooch, preventing further conversation.

Xerxes looked at the pile of books from the previous day and picked up the picture book on JRD Tata, which was right at the top. He flipped to the end of the book, which showed JRD Tata being given numerous national and international awards.

'India's highest civilian awards, Bharat Ratna, Padma Vibhushan,' pronounced Xerxes, with some difficulty. Then he said excitedly, 'Legion of Honour! I didn't know JRD Tata was in the Legion!' As he read further, he discovered that it wasn't what he thought at all. 'Oh, he wasn't part of the superhero series! It's an award of the French government!'

Xerxes lost interest and turned back to the opening pages. He read that JRD Tata was born a French citizen and lived in France during his childhood.

'Chez Tata,' said Xerxes to himself.

Xerxes began to turn the pages more slowly. He spotted a photograph of JRD Tata in his school uniform in the Paris school.

He read aloud, 'His teacher in the Paris school called him "L'Egyptian"—"the Egyptian"—

and he could never understand why! Oh, that sounds just like my classmates!'

Xerxes turned the page and found another photograph of JRD Tata as a boy in a different school uniform.

'He studied in a school in Bombay?' Xerxes counted on his fingers all the places where JRD Tata studied and exclaimed, 'Four places—Paris, Bombay, and later London and Japan!' Xerxes nodded to himself. 'That's why Mama keeps changing my schools! Just like JRD Tata!'

Xerxes got bored of the pictures of all the companies JRD Tata had started. He tried to see how fast he could turn the pages and photographs of an older JRD Tata in other uniforms passed by in a blur.

'Finished!' said Xerxes triumphantly and put the book aside. He looked glumly at the remaining pile of unread books. He didn't want to read any more. He jumped up as he got an idea.

When Grandpa peeked in, Xerxes was walking around with all the books balanced on his head.

Xerxes walked towards him, yelling, 'Bhaaaajiiiwaalaa,' in a singsong voice. 'Do you want some potatoes?' he asked.

'How much?'

'Fifteen rupees a kilo.'

'Too much!'

'It's not.'

'Fifty rupees is too much!'

'Grandpa, I said fifteen, one-five, not fifty!'

'I can't hear properly, I am not your Grandpa. I am Kerentakrous, who refuses to wear his hearing aid to the market for fear it will fall out!'

'Okay, Mr Kerentakrous, I said FIFTEEN. Not FIFTY!'

'Look what you just did!'

'What?!'

'All the potatoes jumped out and ran away because you yelled like that!'

'Oh, that's why my basket feels so light now!'

'Yes. I didn't say I can't hear, I just said I can't hear properly!'

'Sorry, Mr Kerentakrous. Let me just chase my potatoes and I'll sell them to you for a discount for being rude!'

Xerxes darted around the table and scrambled beneath it, reaching out for the imaginary potato. He dashed around as Grandpa shouted out instructions on where to find the rest of them.

'There's another one there, behind the cherry tomatoes, and there goes one holding its nose, jumping over the fish! And that one is hiding behind the plump pumpkin. And look, there's one pretending to be a chikoo!'

Xerxes finally returned to Grandpa, panting from all the running around. Cupping his hands as if carrying something, he presented Grandpa the imaginary potatoes.

'Here are your potatoes for just ten rupees, Mr Kerentakrous.'

But Grandpa turned around and wandered away.

'Hey, sir, Mr Kerentakrous, your potatoes!'

Xerxes followed Grandpa with his arms raised as if carrying his basket.

'Mr Kerentakrous is no more. He died of boredom waiting for your potatoes!'

Xerxes let his arms fall, thought for a while and then cheerily addressed Grandpa.

'Well, then, I'm Millijinipinni, who helps senior citizens. What can I fetch for you, sir?'

'I'd like some fruits, please. I'll point with my walking stick and tell you which to fetch for me.'

Grandpa pointed to a globe.

'I'd like that watermelon.'

'Millijinipinni will get it for you, sir, but state your price.'

'Quarter of whatever it's for!'

'He won't give it for so less!'

'Well, tell him then that I'm a senior citizen and so I am entitled to concessions, including hefty discounts!'

'Okay, sir!'

Xerxes ran to the globe and Grandpa did a quick twirl and ended up behind it as the watermelon seller.

'Watermelon, watermelon, red, juicy, going for thirty!'

'I want it for …'

Xerxes closed his eyes, trying to calculate a quarter of thirty in his head.

'Come on, come on, other customers are waiting, move aside.'

Grandpa tapped Xerxes lightly on the shoulder and addressed an imaginary customer.

'Yes, yes, two for the price of one? Madam, let's make it two for the price of one and a half! Yes? Done.'

He picked up the globe.

Xerxes did a little jump and took it.

'Hey, that's for the lady, no manners!'

'I was the first to come here. And I'm giving you quarter of the price. Here!'

'But that's two watermelons you're walking off with. Come right back here, young man.'

Xerxes returned. Grandpa unscrewed the globe from its stand. He handed over the globe with one hand, took the stand in his other hand and danced out of Xerxes's reach.

'Yes, madam, let me take that and put it in the car,' said Grandpa.

Xerxes made the sound of a car driving up. He tipped his hand at his head, as if doffing his hat like a chauffeur. Taking the stand from Grandpa, he set the globe down on it. Then he pretended it was a car gear and shifting it into reverse, started moving back. He dashed straight into Noshir and dropped the globe. The stand came off.

There was a moment of silence. Then Grandpa lifted the fallen stand and used it like a broom.

'Excuse me, sir, please can you step aside? I have to clean the watermelon squash oozing all over the road.'

'What watermelon! Mamavaji, are you okay?' asked Noshir.

As he stepped forward, Grandpa scowled at him. Xerxes giggled.

'Look, Papa! Your feet are covered with red juice.'

Noshir caught on that it was a game and laughed. He nimbly stepped aside and, pretending to open an imaginary tap, shook one foot and then the other under it to wash them. Xerxes was delighted.

Grandpa shoved the globe and stand to the corner. Then he caught Xerxes around the waist and swinging him around, pushed him ahead of him.

'Spinach, spring onion, radish and purple cabbage, all fresh from the farm on a cart near you!'

'I don't want to be a vegg' Xerxes, struggling out of his grasp

Noshir made a cycling motio of a bicycle bell. 'What am I selling?

Xerxes squealed, 'Ice cream!'

Noshir patted his pockets and found his handkerchief. He pulled it out, and folding it into a cone, presented it to Xerxes.

'Here's a choco cone for you!'

Xerxes pretended to lick the cone.

'Grandpa, it's delicious! Have some!'

Grandpa was standing over Noshir with upraised arms.

'I can't! I'm the awning over the ice-cream vendor's cart.'

Noshir pretended to lick a lolly.

'Well, I'm taking a break in the shade and going to have some of my lolly, too!'

At that moment, Sonji appeared in the doorway. Xerxes licked the last dollop of ice cream off his lips. Noshir did a little skip after finishing his lolly, when he spotted Sonji and froze in mid-action.

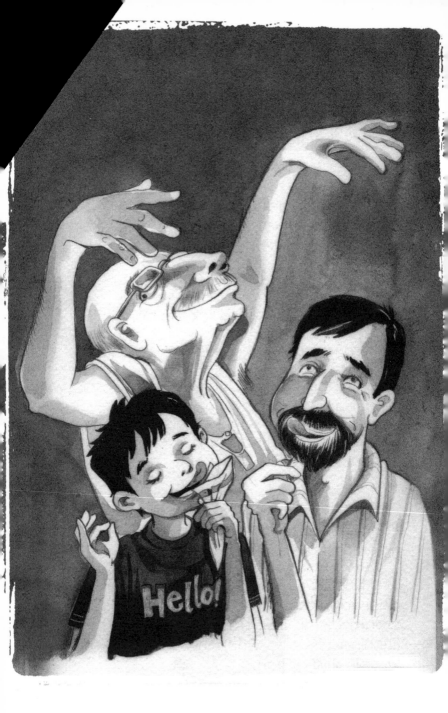

Xerxes looked at her pleadingly, hoping she would join in. But instead, she spoke curtly to his father.

'We have to take Xerxes to the Fire Temple. Isn't that why you came home early? To get him ready?'

Noshir nodded at Xerxes. Grandpa stubbornly remained with his arms in the air. But seeing the others leave, he finally let them fall by his side.

'Do you want to come with us?' asked Sonji.

'No,' said Grandpa, matching her curt tone.

On the way to the Fire Temple, Xerxes chattered away in the back seat of the car as his father drove and Sonji sat next to him.

'It was so much fun, Mama, I chased potatoes, then Mr Kerentakrous died of boredom!'

Sonji jerked back to stare at her son.

'What? What did you just say?'

Xerxes said in a small voice, 'Mr Kerentakrous.'

'After that, what did you say happened to him?'

'He died of boredom!'

Sonji, looking grimly at Noshir, muttered to herself.

'Just had his Navjote! Going to the Fire Temple and he's talking about dying!'

Noshir said nothing. Xerxes chattered on.

'And then Papa came and got watermelon juice all over his feet, no, Papa?'

'Stop distracting your father when he's driving! Tell me what you learned about JRD Tata!'

'Oh, Mama, his mother died when she was just forty-three, and he'd have died, too, in his twenties because being French, he had to join a regiment during World War II, and he got out just in time because they were all killed when they fought in Morocco!' said Xerxes in one breathless rush.

Sonji fumed silently. Noshir looked straight ahead, avoiding her glance. He spotted a policeman ahead.

'Sit back properly, Xerxes. Sonji, put on your seat belt.'

Xerxes slumped back in his seat and the rest of the journey passed in complete silence. A plane flew low overhead and Xerxes sat up and craned his neck, watching it till it vanished from sight.

At night, Xerxes crept into Grandpa's room

to tell him about the aeroplane that he had seen. But Grandpa had gone off to sleep.

Xerxes saw the old family album that Grandpa had shown him earlier, lying on the bedside table. He took it back to his room.

As he turned the pages, he saw a photograph of Grandpa as a young man chatting with a young couple as they all stood outside a cinema hall.

In the background was the little girl whom he now knew to be his mother. She was laughing, and her hands were raised as she played with a young boy whose hands were in a similar pose.

'Mama's playing ice-cream soda with him!' Xerxes exclaimed.

Xerxes sang softly to himself.

Ice-cream soda,
Sugar on the top
Tell me the name of the ice-cream shop
A, B, C, D, E, F, G ....

Then he stopped short and looked closely at the young boy.

'Who is he?'

Xerxes traced his fingers over the young boy's face and then his big ears.

'Oh, this looks like Papa! So are these his parents talking with Grandpa? Let me go and ask!'

He ran with the album to his parents' room but stopped short on hearing his mother's voice.

'Isn't it enough my father is like this that you behave like him?! Xerxes was jumping backwards that day and today you were playing like a kid!! As it is, the neighbours are nosy. What will they think?!'

'In old age, we, too, shall behave like kids, Sonji. Why see it as an illness?'

He heard his mother weeping softly.

Xerxes returned quietly to his room and continued going through the album.

He came across a photograph of a younger Grandpa in uniform. He looked at it closely. Then he opened the JRD Tata book and examined a photograph in it. It showed JRD Tata in uniform standing with his hand outstretched, touching a small aeroplane.

Xerxes read the text beneath the photograph out loud.

'JRD Tata was India's first licensed pilot and started an aviation company, which later became Air India.'

FiVE

On the weekend, Xerxes went to the bakery with his father.

He loved being there most of the time. But sometimes he got bored. He opened the cash drawer and took out a handful of coins.

He scattered the coins all over the counter and tried to get his father to join in his game.

'See, Papa, you have to pick out only the one-rupee coins and make them into piles of five rupees. But fast-fast. Like this!'

Xerxes began building the coin piles. But in his rush to finish, he scattered them even more. Some of the coins rolled over the counter to the floor.

Noshir yelled at him. 'You're not a kid anymore! Your Navjote is over now, behave!'

Xerxes sat sulking till it was time for Noshir to take him home.

Grandpa was making a fuss about eating. Sonji tried to feed him but he kept banging his fork on the table.

Xerxes picked up a spoon. 'Mama, bang the spoon on the table and then Grandpa will enjoy eating and not fuss so much!'

Xerxes began banging the spoon, keeping time with Grandpa's fork. They created quite a racket. Finally, Grandpa began eating with his spoon even as he continued banging the fork with his other hand.

'See, Mama, Grandpa's eating!'

'Okay, but you shouldn't make noise or talk while eating.'

'Why?'

Sonji and Noshir exchanged a look and did not respond.

After lunch, Xerxes went looking for Grandpa. He found him lying flat on his stomach in the garden. He scrambled down on all fours next to him.

'What are you doing, Grandpa?'

Grandpa said nothing. Xerxes kept silent.

Moments passed. Xerxes snuggled down next to Grandpa in the same position. After a while, he heard a 'whoosh' and then water sprayed all around them as Preeti's gardener watered the plants on the other side of the common boundary wall.

Xerxes looked up and saw droplets dancing in the sunlight, filtering through the trees. Grandpa took a deep breath. Xerxes mimicked him and then the fragrance of the moist earth hit him. They stayed there awhile, till the spray stopped.

Grandpa, with his head cushioned in his arms, smiled at Xerxes, who grinned back. Grandpa splayed his arms and raised his head and legs off the ground. He looked like a bird or a plane about to take off.

'Grandpa, since you like flying so much, have you ever flown a plane?'

Grandpa shook his head. Xerxes sighed.

As he wandered back into the house, he heard his parents talking.

'It's time to shift him somewhere else, find a nice home-like institution where he will adjust better. We need to take him out of here. Xerxes will never grow up with his Mamavaji around.'

Xerxes couldn't bear the idea of being put in a boarding school. He had to become JRD Tata, fast!

When Noshir left for the bakery and Sonji retired to her room for a nap, Xerxes scribbled a hurried note for her. He grabbed his satchel and rushed into the garden, where Grandpa was feeding the sparrows.

'Grandpa, Grandpa, come on quick. We have to go!'

He pulled at Grandpa, trying to get him to come with him.

'Arre, but tell me what, where do we have to go!'

'You just come, no.'

Xerxes and Grandpa trotted out of the gate, and Xerxes hailed a passing cab.

'Where to?' asked the driver.

Grandpa looked at Xerxes for the answer.

'I don't know, but I can give you directions.'

'It's not too far, is it? I have to return the taxi in an hour.'

Xerxes just nodded and bundled Grandpa into the taxi. They reached the area where he had spotted the plane, when they were driving to the Fire Temple.

'Here, take a right turn.'

The taxi driver protested.

'You have to tell me where exactly you want to go. If it's a dead-end lane, we'll be stuck.'

'Well, I saw a plane ...'

'You saw a plane?! We all see planes. Don't tell me you're chasing some plane! Is this some silly mobile game of yours?'

Grandpa intervened. 'Listen, he doesn't even have a mobile phone! If you let him complete his sentence instead of rudely interrupting, he'll tell us!'

'You mean even you don't know where he's headed!'

'Come on Xerxes, we'll walk the rest of the way! This guy is in no mood to take us where you want!'

They paid off the cabbie and trotted off. After walking past dumpsters and dilapidated houses, Grandpa finally ventured to ask.

'Really, I must ask now, Xerxes, where are we going?'

'The other day I saw a plane flying low somewhere here. There must be an airfield.'

'Why didn't you just tell the taxi driver that, then? The flight path of a plane is not the same as the road, you know! We could be wandering around for hours!'

'Grandpa, please, why don't you just see it as an adventure?'

'An adventure?!'

'Yes. If we could make up a market at home that day, why can't we imagine we're not here but someplace else?'

'Such as?'

'Gootchputcha Phata!'

'And what is that?'

'That is the lane where once upon a time merchants sold velvet. The entire phata would be draped in velvet so that when people walked on it their feet would land softly.'

'But then why call it Gootchputcha? Why not Velvetiana?'

'Because Gootchputcha sounds like ghoospoos—people in Gootchputcha spoke in whispers as soft as the velvet they sold in secret.'

'Why was it secret?'

'Only a few knew how to make it. They didn't want others to know, because then they could get robbed.'

'So, if they were to call it Velvetiana, then people would come to know where it is being sold!'

'Yes, Grandpa, now you get it!'

'But if people stepped on it, surely they would know?'

'No, they wouldn't. The velvet covering the road was so lovely and smooth that people walking over it were hypnotised and thought they were floating through clouds. And that it was all a dream.'

'I hope this airfield of yours is not a dream!'

'Grandpa, you're not enjoying this at all. I thought it would make you happy, being out on your own.'

'I don't know, Xerxes. I'm old now and I'm afraid of being out and about like this. We didn't even tell your parents and we don't have a mobile phone!'

'Grandpa, don't worry! I left a note at home telling Mama we'll be back soon!'

'But did you say where?'

'No,' Xerxes admitted.

'I think your Mama's going to have a fit!'

'All right then, let's go back.'

Grandpa saw Xerxes's sad face.

'Okay, let's make a deal. If we don't reach this airfield of yours in the next two minutes, we'll turn back. Okay?'

'Okay Grandpa! If you're tired, I'll just go a bit ahead and check. Why don't you sit on this scooter seat till then?'

'No, no, Xerxes, please don't go off anywhere like that, leaving me alone.'

Hearing his worried tone, Xerxes held Grandpa's hand tight and they both started walking slowly. They heard the sound of the scooter starting up. Turning back, they approached the scooterist.

'Excuse me, ma'am, could you please tell us if there's an airfield somewhere here?'

'Sure, there is—just two minutes away.'

Xerxes clapped his hands in delight. 'See, Grandpa, just two minutes!'

The scooterist smiled and said, 'I meant two minutes on wheels.'

Xerxes looked pleadingly at Grandpa.

'Since it's a short distance, please could you give us a ride?'

'Hop on.'

Xerxes stood behind the handle bars and Grandpa took the pillion seat behind the scooterist.

Sonji found the note with Xerxes's childish scrawl and called Noshir.

'He's written, "Dear Mama, I and Mamavaji ..." It should be Mamavaji and I, why can't he get it right! Okay, okay, Noshir, don't get irritated! I'm reading it out: "... I and Mamavaji are out for a while. We will be back soon. Xerxes." No, he hasn't written where. No, I don't have a clue! All right, I'm not panicking, I'm just informing you he left a note. Yes, we'll wait and see. Bye.'

SiX

Xerxes and Grandpa walked into a building near the small airfield. A young man was seated behind a tall desk. A small board next to him said, 'Receptionist'.

'Sir, please could you tell me how I can become a pilot?'

Looking slightly puzzled, the receptionist replied to Grandpa, thinking he had posed the question.

'Sir, you'll need to show a fitness certificate, first.'

'What is that?'

The receptionist suddenly realised that the voice was coming from behind his tall desk. He peered over and spotted Xerxes.

'Ah,' he said, sounding relieved. 'I was wondering how an old man was speaking in a child's voice. So, little man, you're the one who wants to become a pilot, is it?'

'Yes!'

'Well, you need to grow up to be eighteen years old.'

Xerxes counted on his fingers and stamped his foot in frustration.

'That's soooo long away!'

'Well, you can start studying. You have to do well in physics and maths.'

'Physics and maths! What's physics?'

'It's one of the science subjects.'

'But why physics and maths?'

'You have to apply that knowledge to become a pilot. So, you need to pass your twelfth exams with at least fifty percent in physics and maths.'

'Fifty percent?!'

'Yes, that's the minimum.'

Xerxes looked glum as an image of his marksheet flashed in his mind. Science: forty percent. Maths: thirty-five percent.

He brightened up as a grey-haired man wearing a pilot's uniform came out of a room and called out to the receptionist.

'I'll just pop down to the canteen for some tea and be back in time for the class.'

Xerxes addressed the receptionist.

'Can Grandpa become a pilot?'

Grandpa was startled.

'As I said earlier, he'll need a fitness certificate from a doctor to be eligible. That means he has to be medically certified as healthy enough to be able to fly a plane.'

'Excuse us for a minute, sir.'

Grandpa took Xerxes aside. 'You didn't ask me if I wanted to become a pilot!'

'Oh, but Mama didn't ask me either whether I want to become JRD Tata!'

'I don't understand what you're saying, Xerxes!'

'See, Grandpa, it's like maths. One plus one is two. I want to be you. But Mama wants me to become JRD Tata. But it'll take me too long! So, you have to become JRD Tata.'

'And how am I supposed to do that?'

'By becoming a pilot, like JRD Tata.'

'I won't pass the medical test!'

'We'll ask for concession, like you did in the market game that day!'

Xerxes scooted back to the receptionist.

'Sir, senior citizens always get concessions. So, can he bunk the medical test?'

The receptionist hid a smile. 'No, sorry!'

Then Xerxes spotted a photograph on the wall behind the desk. It looked like the cockpit of a plane, but it was inside a room!

'What is that?' Xerxes asked the receptionist.

'That's our training facility.'

'Can Grandpa at least sit in that and have his photo taken?'

'No. It's not allowed. Only pilots are allowed.' Then he winked at Grandpa. 'But we could give him a concession for that! We have a bit of time since the pilot trainer has gone out.'

He pointed them to the room and Xerxes rushed towards it, dragging Grandpa behind him. He squealed in delight seeing the aeroplane cockpit.

'See, Grandpa, just like in a plane.'

The receptionist came in and hoisted Xerxes into the cockpit. He invited Grandpa to take the other seat.

'Here you are, in the cockpit. We use it to train pilots to give them a feel of the instruments needed during the flight. It's called simulating the experience and this contraption is therefore a …?'

'Simulation!'

'Well, it's called a simulator. But yes, it does simulation!'

Grandpa looked at Xerxes quizzically.

'What, Grandpa?'

'You said you wanted to take a photograph?'

Xerxes stuck out his tongue and slapped his head. 'Oh, yes, I forgot about that!'

The young man looked at Grandpa and said, 'You can click it on your mobile.'

Grandpa shook his head. 'I don't have one.'

Xerxes made a great show of looking through his pockets. There was nothing in them. Then he slipped his hand into his satchel and came up with the polaroid camera. Xerxes chortled at Grandpa's expression.

'Fooled you, Grandpa!'

'Who gave you that?'

'Mama! For my class presentation.'

Xerxes handed over the camera to the receptionist.

'Sir, please could you take a photograph of Grandpa?'

'Only Grandpa?'

'One of Grandpa, one of me and one of both of us. Please.'

The receptionist clicked their photographs. As the photographs swished out one after the other, Xerxes checked them all to see they had come out properly.

'Satisfied?'

Young men and women could be seen entering the gates of the building.

'Okay, we have to leave now,' said the receptionist. 'The class is about to begin.'

Xerxes thanked the receptionist and made sure to keep the camera back carefully in his satchel. He scrambled out and rushed to the other side to help Grandpa climb out.

They left the building and hailed a taxi. As they rode towards home, Xerxes thought about what he had found out.

'If I fail in science and maths, I can't become a pilot,' he told Grandpa.

'If I don't become a pilot, maybe, I'll sit in the bakery, and will learn to do business like Papa.'

'You don't want to become like Mama—a vet?'

'No, Grandpa, Mama wants me to become JRD Tata so either I become a pilot or I start a business!'

On the way back home, they stopped to take copies of the cockpit photographs and a photocopy of the old photograph from the family album, showing Grandpa in uniform, that Xerxes had been carrying carefully in his satchel.

SEVEN

Sonji heard the sound of the taxi and rushed to the gate as Grandpa and Xerxes alighted.

'Where had you gone?'

'Gootchputcha!' said Grandpa. Xerxes giggled.

'What?'

'Come on, Sonji, we just went out for a spin.'

'But where?'

'Here and there.'

'Xerxes, you tell me. Where did you go with Mamavaji?'

'He didn't go with Mamavaji, did you, Xerxes? Mamavaji went with you!'

Grandpa winked at Xerxes and they

marched into the house beating imaginary drums.

Sonji called Noshir. 'They're home but refuse to say where they went! Yes, I'll try and ask later and see.'

While Grandpa watched TV, Sonji sat down for a chat with Xerxes when she brought him his soup.

'Did you have fun with Mamavaji today?'

Xerxes nodded.

'It was thoughtful of you to leave the note but it would have been better if you'd let me know before heading out.'

Xerxes remained silent and slurped his soup with great concentration.

'So, where is Gootchputcha?'

Xerxes pointed to his soup.

'What? It's a soup place?'

Xerxes shook his head.

'Then? What are you saying, do speak up!'

'You only told me I should not talk while eating! And you were sleeping when we left so I left a note.'

'Okay, but where did you go?'

Xerxes raised his eyebrows at his soup.

'Right! I'll wait till you've finished.'

Sonji waited for Xerxes to finish his soup but he made such slow going of it that she eventually gave up and left him to it. Xerxes hid a smile.

Sonji was in her clinic attending to a dog, Rufus, who was limping from a wound. Suddenly, Rufus gave a low growl.

Sonji glanced up and saw the clinic door that was opening slowly, shut abruptly. She finished up with Rufus and let him out through the back door. There was a car waiting and Rufus got in through the window. A man in a white uniform and peaked cap came running.

'Oh, Dr Sonji, that was quick.'

'It was just a surface wound. Bye, Rufus.'

Rufus barked his thanks and the car drove off. Sonji went back in.

'Rufus is gone, Papa. You can come in.'

Sonji knew that animals frisking around unnerved her father. So, she wondered why he'd ventured to her clinic. Grandpa shuffled inside.

'What brings you here, Papa?'

'I just wanted to ask you why you want Xerxes to become like JRD Tata.'

Sonji put her hands on her hips.

'Why did you name me Sonji?'

Grandpa did a right-about turn and was out of the door like a shot. He knew when he was beaten in an argument before it had even started!

Sonji hid a smile and looked just like Xerxes. She pranced out happily and later in the evening, laughed as she shared it with Noshir.

'Papa just r-a-a-a-n away when I mentioned his naming me Sonji!'

Noshir was busy trying to fix back the plastic cover on the dial of his watch and was barely paying attention. But he nodded dutifully because he had heard the same story from Sonji a thousand times before.

'Mama wanted to name me Sooni but Papa insisted on Sonji because that was his idol, the boxer Muhammad Ali's wife's name! And wherever I went everyone would go on and on about it. "Oh, Sonji, that's not a Parsi name, is it?" they'd all titter.'

Noshir managed to fix the cover back. He held the watch to his ear to ensure it was still working.

'It's only when I was with Papa that people would accept that yes, I am a Parsi!'

Noshir completed the line for her, 'And then they'd say, "Oh, you have a Parsi nose", whatever that meant!'

Sonji grinned at his intervention. Seeing that she was in a good mood, Noshir ventured to ask her the question that had yet to get an answer.

'But why *do* you want Xeroo to be like Jeh?' asked Noshir, using the diminutive form of JRD Tata's name, Jehangir, as if he had been on first-name basis with him.

'His French mother Suzanne changed her name to Sooni after she married a Parsi! And she was the first woman in India to drive a car and her son piloted India's first commercial flight! My Xeroo should be like him, first at something!'

'Oh,' said Noshir. 'But we are all already firsts in our respective families, aren't we? Each of us is the first and only child!'

Sonji would have none of it.

'Oh, Noshir, almost all Parsis are! I want him to stand out at something!'

When the entire family went to the Fire Temple the next day, Xerxes said a little prayer.

'Please, please may Ahura Mazda get me at least fifty percent in science and maths.'

Sonji overheard him telling Grandpa about what he'd prayed for. She repeated it to Noshir with delight.

'Our Xeroo is finally showing some ambition. He wants to improve his science and maths grades. He's getting interested in science!'

The following day, instead of dropping off Xerxes at the bakery after school, as he was expecting her to do, Sonji stopped the car at another house and took Xerxes in with his schoolbag.

A lady came forward.

'Oh, Sonji, so wonderful to see you! So, this is your boy!'

Sonji nudged Xerxes, who introduced himself.

'Xerxes, you'll be starting your tuitions with me today,' the lady declared. 'To help you improve your marks in science and maths!'

At night, Xerxes sobbed into his pillow.

'I asked to improve my marks, not get a tuition teacher! Now I have no time to go to Papa's bakery and to play with Grandpa!'

When Sonji came to wake him the following morning, he felt hot to her touch.

'Noshir!'

Noshir came quickly.

'He's got fever. I'll stay home with him today.'

'I'll call the school bus teacher and inform her he's not coming.'

When Xerxes awoke, it was nearly noon. He could hear his parents in the kitchen.

'I'll do it, Noshir. You take some rest.'

'No, it's okay. I'll cut these; you want me to toss the leeks in with the rice?'

'No, I've put the rice in the cooker. I'll heat some turmeric milk for Xerxes.'

Seeing Sonji occupied, Grandpa came to sit with Xerxes.

'Hey, what happened to you?'

'Grandpa, nothing has happened to me. I just need to rest as I've been thinking too much.'

'About what?'

'Finding a short cut.'

'Well, I do hope you know where exactly to, or you'll end up walking too much, like that day!'

'There's no such thing as walking too much!'

'Get to my age and you'll see!'

'Grandpa, why don't you get to my age? You'll be able to pass science and maths with better marks than me.'

'I don't want to study any more. These are my days of childhood—no studying!'

'What are you saying, Grandpa? I don't understand but I know you can pass with good grades without studying!'

'And how is that?'

'You make up so many wonderful things!'

'Your teacher doesn't want imaginative answers but correct answers. What will I do then?'

'I wish I knew.'

'There you go again, thinking too much! Chalo, I better leave you alone before your Mama says ...'

At that moment, Sonji yelled, 'Papa, let him sleep, don't go chitter-chatter.'

Grandpa grinned and left as Sonji came in with turmeric milk for Xerxes.

When Noshir came to check on Xerxes later, he found him fast asleep, with the JRD Tata book next to him. The book was open at a page with a photograph of JRD Tata as a pilot. Xerxes stirred, and still half-asleep, muttered multiplication tables. Noshir patted him back to sleep and went to speak to Sonji.

'I think it's best not to send Xeroo for tuitions. He's not able to cope.'

'He didn't fall ill because he went for tuitions, and that too just one day! It's because Papa took him for an outing in the heat! Without hats, too!'

'Sonji, please, don't keep blaming your father for everything that happens to Xerxes!'

But Sonji was already going towards Grandpa's room. Noshir shook his head as he heard her scold Grandpa for taking Xerxes out in the heat. Grandpa said nothing and just looked down sadly.

Xerxes heard it all and had a feverish dream in which the photograph of JRD Tata in the book dissolved and became Grandpa wearing the uniform.

EIGHT

Xerxes was ill for several days.

On his first day of school after the long absence, Sonji picked Xerxes up from school and dropped him off at the gate, while she went around the lane to park the car.

Xerxes saw Preeti Aunty coming out of her house with her arms full of sacks.

'Hello, Xerxes, so you're back from school. Good to see you've recovered.'

'Would you like me to help you, Aunty?'

'No, dear, but do come, and tell the others. We're about to start our fete!'

'What is that?'

'Just going to have fun and games.'

'Games?!'

'Yes, there's one for senior citizens, too. That's what these sacks are for. Tell Mamavaji!'

Xerxes darted into the house and flung his bag on the table. Yelling at Noshir that he was going out, he rushed out of the room before his father could say anything. When Noshir followed him, he saw Xerxes impatiently hopping on one foot and then the other as Grandpa made him wear a cap.

'Come on, Grandpa, we have to go! The race is going to start.'

Sonji came back after parking the car and heard him. 'You're not going anywhere, Xerxes, come right back inside. You've just recovered from fever, I won't have …'

But Xerxes was off at a run. Noshir followed, to bring him back.

'Papa, why didn't you make him sit in the house?! He's just recovered! He's bound to catch something in this crowd!'

Sonji realised that she was talking to air. Grandpa had also vanished.

Sonji made her way towards the crowd that had gathered in the open ground in the colony, muttering all the way.

Noshir had already reached the ground, and spotted Grandpa and Xerxes.

Grandpa was practising holding the sack for the sack race. 'I can't hold it tight, Xerxes.'

Xerxes went to Grandpa and showed him what to do.

'See, Grandpa, wrap it around your wrists at either end and then even if your grip slips, you will still be holding on to it.'

Sonji scanned the crowd and spotted Noshir, who gestured to her. She looked in the direction he was pointing.

The sack race was on. Wildly cheered on by Xerxes, Grandpa was jumping ahead in a sack. He reached the finish line in first position.

'Grandpa won! Grandpa won!' exulted Xerxes to his parents. He showed them the photo of Grandpa winning the race that he had clicked on the polaroid camera.

'Give me that. You must not be out, Xerxes, you know that. Come on back home.'

Seeing Noshir and Sonji, Preeti pulled them forward.

'Come on, come on, your turn next, Noshir!'

'We really must get back, my son's just recovered from his illness.'

'Oh, yes, I met him when he came back from school! He's fit as a fiddle. And look at Mamavaji, no one would believe he's a senior citizen!'

She handed Noshir a lemon and spoon and pushed him to the starting line. He started the race but stopped mid-way, embarrassed at the idea of running with a lemon and spoon in front of Sonji.

Grandpa yelled at him. 'You can't stop in the middle like that! It's a race! Finish it!'

Xerxes hollered, 'You can't give up, Papa!'

Hearing them, Noshir picked up his pace and came in third.

An announcement boomed out over the megaphone.

'A Grand Prize for the family if every member of the family wins in a race! The next race needs two members of a family for each team!'

Sonji perked up and catching Xerxes's hand, she rushed to the start of the balloon race and explained it to him.

'See, Xerxes, those balloons along the string. You have to blow them up for me and I will run with them to the finish line turn by turn.'

The race began. Xerxes blew up the first balloon and quickly handed it over to Sonji.

'Go, Mama, go.'

Sonji was the first to reach the finish line with a balloon. She quickly turned back for the next.

Noshir and Grandpa tried to outshout each other, cheering Sonji and Xerxes.'Come on, Sonji. He's already finished with the second one!' 'Run, run!'

Xerxes blew up the balloons and Sonji ran to the finish line with them, and back.

'Last one, Mama, fast, fast.'

Sonji saw another mother was racing ahead of her.

Grandpa yelled, 'Run, Sonji. You've to be faster than that!'

Sonji ran and overtook her competitor, but in her haste, she burst the balloon in her hand.

But everyone gathered around Xerxes and Sonji at the finish line.

'Congrats, Sonji, Xerxes! That was a wonderful pace you set. And even though you came in second, you won the Grand Prize!'

Preeti said, 'No wonder you ran so fast in the race, Sonji! Just like your father was faster than everyone else in the sack race!'

Sonji grinned.

Grandpa and Noshir pushed their way through the crowd.

'Oh, hello, the two of us also deserve the congratulations.'

Xerxes screamed, 'We won, Grandpa, we won!'

Grandpa pumped his fists in the air in jubilation.

Preeti shook Grandpa's hand. 'Yes, Mamavaji, you were really good. The best. Where do you get all that energy from?'

'Keep laughing!'

Everyone laughed and shook hands with Grandpa. He beamed proudly as their praise poured in.

'That was great …'

'You were super, Mamavaji …'

'I've taken a video and I'm going to send it to my father to show him he can still be active at this age, too!'

At that moment, Preeti called out. 'Okay, okay, we have to present the Grand Prize now. Please make some space.'

The Grand Prize envelope was handed over to Grandpa, who handed it to Sonji.

'Thank you, thank you.'

Xerxes nudged Sonji. 'Mama, let's take a group photo.'

Sonji gave the polaroid camera to Preeti. 'Please take a family photo.'

'Okay, say cheese!'

After everyone dispersed, Sonji opened the envelope to check what they'd won. Her face fell as she saw the gift coupon.

Noshir noticed her expression. 'What's the matter?'

Sonji pointed to the banners; the sponsors of the fete were makers of kitchen appliances.

'I was hoping to get one of those. But this gift coupon is for books!'

Noshir grinned. Sonji didn't understand why. 'What's so funny?'

'Now you know what Xerxes felt like when he got just books when he wanted toys for his Navjote!!'

Sonji broke into a smile and then she started laughing, too. Xerxes watched her merriment in wonder, and realised that she looked just as she had in the photograph in the old family album, laughing as she played the ice-cream soda game. Grandpa had wandered off, so Noshir went to look for him.

Xerxes nodded to himself and tapped their family group photograph.

'Chez Wadia,' he said softly.

'What did you say, Xerxes?' asked Sonji.

'Chez Wadia. We can stay together now.'

'Yes, we do stay together.'

'You were going to send me to boarding.'

'Who was sending you to boarding?'

'You were. I heard you. You spoke of sending me away to a home-like place.'

'Oh, Xerxes, it wasn't you we were talking of sending away ...'

Sonji's voice trailed off. Xerxes stared at her and stamped his foot in anger.

'No, no, you can't send Grandpa to boarding! He was better than all of us today, he won!'

'It's not that, Xerxes.'

But Xerxes ran off, angry tears rolling down his face.

'Wait, Xerxes, listen to me!'

Xerxes did not stop. Noshir and Grandpa, having cold coffee from the vending machine, did not notice him as he ran past them all the way home. Sonji found him huddled up in his room.

'We aren't sending either of you anywhere, Xeroo. We changed our minds that very day, when Mamavaji and you went off to Gootchputcha all by yourselves! And today, you saw what a crowd there was, but your Mamavaji managed on his own, didn't he?'

Xerxes fished out his notebook and showed her a page in it.

'See, Mama, I can manage, too.'

Sonji saw that it had the photograph of Xerxes standing with his hand outstretched, touching the cockpit where Grandpa was seated. He had stuck his own photograph over a photocopy of Grandpa's old photograph so that it seemed as if Xerxes was wearing a uniform.

'See, Mama, I can grow up to be just like JRD Tata in that book! And also be like Grandpa!'

Xerxes had scrawled behind the photograph.

When I Grow Up I Want to Be Like JRD Mamavaji Tata.

Sonji smiled and gave Xerxes a big hug.

Madhuri Kamat has documented and edited NGO work for two decades, written a poem on women who live on the pavement, a play on child sexual abuse and a script for UNICEF, and translated poems by street children. She has penned television soaps and scripts for forthcoming films. Her first book is *Whose Father, What Goes?*, a retelling of *Hamlet*.

Niloufer Wadia quit her advertising career of over twenty years to follow her true love, illustration and painting. Happening upon children's book illustration by chance in 2016, she now has published over fifteen storybooks, with several more in the pipeline. Besides this, she illustrates book covers, sketches regularly, does some cartooning and paints on canvas when no deadlines hound her.